Contents

Cover illustration by David Pattison

Published by Ladybird Books Ltd
80 Strand London WC2R 0RL
A Penguin Company

10

ISBN-13: 978-0-72142-388-3
Printed in China

Whoops, there go my trousers!

written by Shirley Jackson

illustrated by David Pattison

On Monday, we did some baking.

On Tuesday, we did some painting.

On Wednesday, we played football. All our trousers had to go in the wash.

On Thursday, we had
to do some writing.

Whoops!

My trousers!

On Friday, we went running through the mud.

On Saturday, my brother
and I went swimming.

On Sunday, Mum did the washing.

Whoops!

There go **my** trousers!

Rainbow's refusal

written by Marie Birkinshaw

illustrated by David Parkins

Emma liked her horse,
Rainbow.

But sometimes Rainbow was naughty. Sometimes he would not do as he was told.

One day the instructor said,
"Walk on."

All the other horses began
to walk.

But Rainbow stayed where he was.

"Trot," said the instructor, and all the other horses began to trot.

But Rainbow stayed where
he was.

"Turn left," said the instructor.

Before Emma could stop him, Rainbow turned right.

"Turn right," said the instructor.

Before Emma could stop him, Rainbow turned left.

"Jump," said the instructor.

But Rainbow stayed where
he was.

All the other horses jumped, and all their riders fell in some wet, sticky mud.

Good old Rainbow!

This time, Emma was glad
that Rainbow hadn't
done as he
was told.

Asleep
all day

written by Marie Birkinshaw

illustrated by Andy DaVolls

Sleep, sleep!
The owls hide away.

Sleep, sleep!
There's no time for play.

Sleep, sleep!
The mouse in a hole.

Sleep, sleep!
Bat,

badger,

mole.

Sleep, sleep!
Away from the light.

Sleep, sleep!
Until it is night.

In the pond

written by Marie Birkinshaw

illustrated by David Pace

I went to the pond.
I could see some eggs.

I went to the pond again.
I could see that the eggs
had turned into tadpoles.

When I went again,
the tadpoles had two legs,

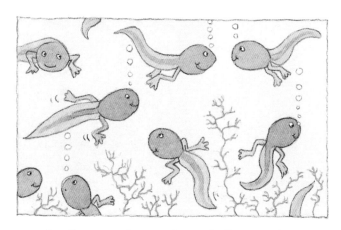

and then they had four legs.

But when I went to the pond again, the tadpoles weren't there.

The pond was full of frogs!

Frog Facts

Frogs are *amphibians*. This means that they spend much of their lives in water as well as on land.

Frogs lay eggs. This is called *spawning*. The eggs hatch into tadpoles, which look like tiny fish.

Tadpoles grow their back legs first, and then their front legs.

When a tadpole changes into a frog, this is called *metamorphosis*.

Frogs have very long, sticky tongues which they use to catch flies and other insects.

Frogs that live in rainforests lay their eggs in damp leaves to keep them moist.

The poison arrow frog lives in rainforests. It is brightly coloured. This tells other animals that it is poisonous.